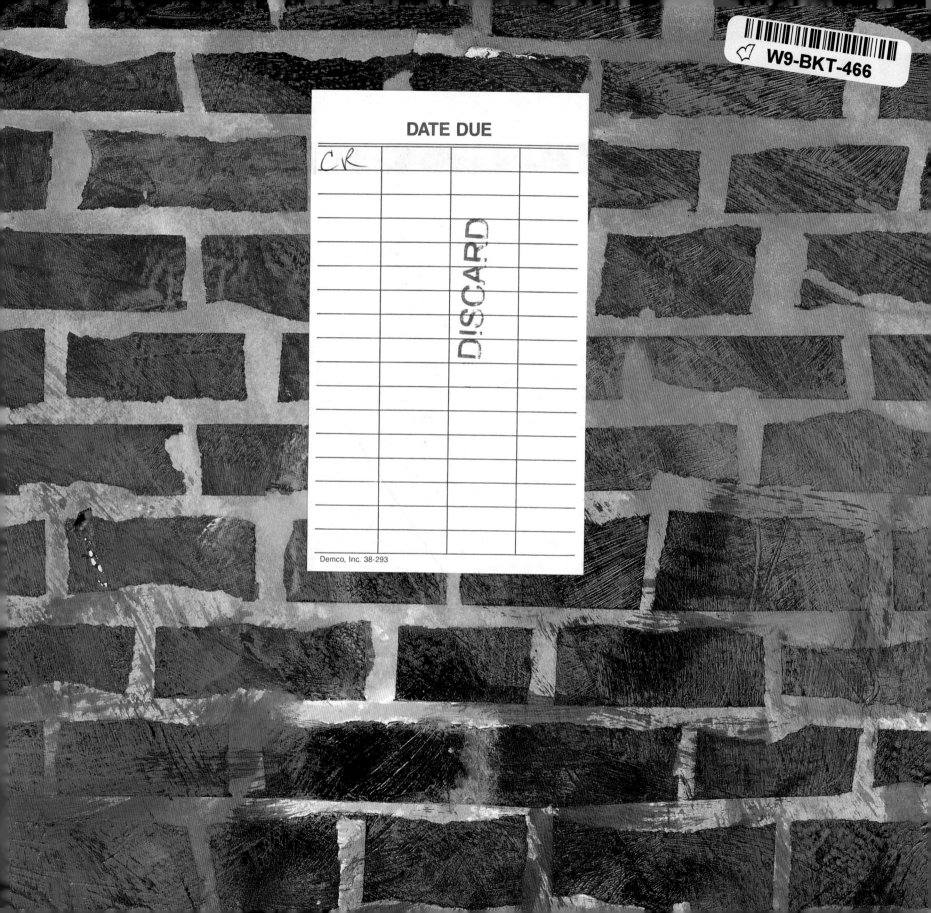

WHITE WASH

by
NTOZAKE SHANGE
Illustrated by
MICHAEL SPORN

Walker and Company
New York

I remember that day so clearly, almost like any other day. Almost.

I was fooling around in class with my best friend, Crystal, when Ms. Steinberg called on me.

"Helene-Angel, what do you think the answer is?"

I didn't even know the question, so I guessed, "Multiply or divide." I figured it's got to be one or the other, right? Everybody but Ms. Steinberg laughed and made faces at me. Oh, I can feel my face going red now just thinking about it.

"One hundred percent of this class multiplied by many days in detention will be the answer if you don't behave." Ms. Steinberg was laughing at her own joke by the time the bell rang. Seeing our chance to escape, we all hurried for the door.

I was the only one in my group who had to wait for a big brother to walk me home. I had to wait for Mauricio every day.

But I didn't complain too much, even though my classmates teased me about being a preschooler. I couldn't say much because Mauricio was not crazy about me tagging along, either.

Soon as I saw him, I fell in step behind him—so I wouldn't be mistaken for his girl, you know.

Mauricio was never satisfied, though. He was still mean to me. He hardly looked at me. Maybe that's why he didn't see the Hawks begin to surround us.

They called us "mud people." One asked if we spoke English, pushing my brother out of the way.

I heard Mauricio shouting to me: "Run! Run, Helene-Angel! Run now!" But how could I? I was scared to death.

I only remember a little of it. Something about doing me a good deed, then about "how to be white" or "American." I don't know. I just know for sure I felt this stinging cold on my face and around my ears and neck.

I was dripping white. Really itchy, stinging white paint covered me wherever my brown skin used to be. I couldn't understand. Why were these boys doing this to me? Why were they laughing as they walked away?

I didn't move. I thought maybe if I sat still all this would stop or disappear. I tried to rub some of the white stuff off, but then my hands turned white, too. I felt like I'd been sitting there forever when I heard Mauricio say, "I'm gonna take you home, Helene-Angel. Okay? Don't be scared now." I thought he had left me there.

Mauricio seemed stunned, but that didn't stop him from lifting my shaking body in his arms. As he walked he tried to hold his head away from mine. I thought he didn't want the "white" stuff to rub off on him. But then I saw what they did to his face. We didn't-couldn't-talk. He carried me home in silence, every so often wiping my tears.

Grandma didn't say much when we got home. She had that sorrowful look on her face that she used to get when she told me about the beat-up, bleeding black children she had seen in the South. But even she'd never seen a colored child painted white.

She kept muttering under her breath words she swore decent people didn't say as she tried to scrub off all the damage. Mauricio tried to slink out of the room, but Grandma made him lie down. "There was nothing more you could do, boy. You were outnumbered."

That didn't sit well with Mauricio, but I don't really remember much from there on. I went into my room and disappeared. Grandma said all the paint was gone, but I could still see it. I could still taste fear in the back of my throat. I could only make those terrible stinging feelings go away by pretending I was a statue. I sat as still as stone.

I could still hear, though. "BLACK GIRL TERRORIZED!" "SPRAY PAINT VICTIM!" "WHITE FOR A DAY!"

I couldn't block the newspaper boys shouting, the neighbors talking, the radio announcing. Mauricio defending me like nothing bad happened to him. For a week I would not come out of my room.

Grandma left me food by my door. She whispered sweet things to me.

That I was beautiful. I was a hero of the race. A brave girl.

Finally, by Monday morning, she said, "Helene-Angel, I don't care who did what to you. Today you are going to open this door and be strong."

I knew by the sound of her voice that I would have to come out of my room. But I could never go back to school. Anybody could see that I was an embarrassment to myself, my friends, the whole world, the universe.

I opened the door, but instead of Grandma, I saw my friends smiling at me.

"We missed you so much!" Crystal said and hugged me. She was crying. Raphael said, "If we all stick together, no one will dare bother you or anybody else, right?"

Before I could think of an answer, I was swept out onto the street surrounded by my classmates. I turned and saw my big brother way down the block, like a dog with his tail between his legs.

I called back, "C'mon, Mauricio." He looked at Grandma, who waved him on. I waited for him to catch up. Then I grabbed his hand and said, "You know, we've got a right to be here, too."

To my wondrous daughter Savannah Thulani-Eloisa that you
may paint the world as you see it. —N. S.

I would like to thank Bridget Thorne and Jason McDonald
for their enormous assistance in preparing the illustrations. —M. S.

First published in the United States of America in 1997 by Walker Publishing Company, Inc.

Published simultaneously in Canada by Thomas Allen & Son Canada Limited, Markham, Ontario

Library of Congress Cataloging-in-Publication Data
Shange, Ntozake.
   Whitewash/by Ntozake Shange; illustrated by Michael Sporn.
   p.   cm.
   Summary: A young African-American girl is traumatized when a gang attacks her and her brother
   on their way home from school and spray paints her face white.
   ISBN 0-8027-8490-9 (hc).—ISBN 0-8027-8491-7 (rein.)
1. Afro-Americans–Juvenile Fiction. [1. Afro-Americans–Fiction. 2. Prejudices–Fiction.] I. Sporn, Michael, ill. II. Title.
PZ7.S52835Wh 1997
[E] - Dc21
                                97-8184
                                CIP
                                AC

Book design by Marva J. Martin

Printed in Hong Kong

10 9 8 7 6 5 4 3 2 1